Piteo and his friend's adventures from the Azores to their forever homes

Linda Spencer

ISBN: 9798527276480

Cover art by Dreamstime

Chapter One
Piteo meets Siel

Piteo was roaming the warm dusty streets of the Azores, unkempt and hungry. He was only four months old, still a puppy and yet, already he felt incredibly old and tired. He was a beautiful little boy with no place to call a home. Sadly, he was kicked out by his owners when he was just a puppy. He felt so sad. They did not know that he had feelings too, that he would miss them.

He was very scared walking around on his own, if a car or bicycle sped by, he would shake like a jelly and cower to the floor, until they had passed before he would begin his search again for food and water.

The main purpose of his day was to survive. There were a lot of big street dogs roaming around, some of them looked truly angry. He would run away and hide.

His whole world felt extremely dangerous to him, he had no one to make him feel safe.

Piteo did not know who he could trust. So, he learned to trust no-one. People walked by him, some would stop and stroke him, then carry on with their daily chores. Some would walk right on by, as if he were invisible, without so much as a glance. He did not trust dogs or humans. He felt very unsafe. He was very lonely. Until one day his life changed.

As he was roaming around minding his own business, he met a doggy called Siel, who was not too scary as he was about the same size as Piteo. Siel stopped in the street and looked at him. Piteo lowered his eyes. He had learned from the other street doggies that if you did not look directly at another dog, it was letting them know that you did not want to fight. Boy he did not want to fight.

"Hey buddy, you want to play" Siel asked.

Piteo just stood there, he could not open his mouth. He wasn't even sure that Siel was actually talking to him, as his name wasn't buddy. He was very shy, but his tail did begin to wag slightly. His tail was out of his control, it had a mind of its own he had thought.

"Lost your voice buddy" Siel asked, with an air of confidence.

"My name is Piteo" he replied squeakily.

"Nice to meet you Piteo" Siel said, "Hey come to the park with me, there is loads to do."

Siel started to walk away. Piteo stood still, his tail still wagged but his body which also seemed to have a mind of its own froze, he could not move even though he wanted to.

"Come on buddy" Siel shouts.

Why does he keep calling me buddy, Piteo thought?

He slowly built up the courage to follow Siel hoping that wherever he was going there would be food. He was so hungry. The last time he had eaten anything was over twelve hours ago. It was only half a stale pepperoni pizza slice that some human had thrown on the pavement. It is surprising how tasty stale food can be when you are hungry. Luckily there had been some rain in the Azores, so he was able to have a drink too!

After about four hundred and forty-four steps they arrived at a park. Piteo always counted his steps because he found that it helped him with his anxiety. Piteo had never seen this place before. It was so green. The soft grass felt so nice against his paws, not rough like the pavements. The smell was different too, so much fresher than the streets.

There were other dogs on the park too, they seemed happier than the street dogs.

"I like it here" he thought to himself keeping one eye on Siel as he did not quite trust him yet.

Siel and Piteo spent most of the day together exploring, what seemed to be a massive green space, with trees and flowers and happy people. Soon Piteo began to trust Siel. They both ran around the park, stopping sometimes to roll in the grass feeling the warm sun tickle their bellies.

Piteo laughed and laughed. He could not remember having so much fun. Siel would crack doggie jokes to make him laugh some more.

"Why do dogs run in circles, buddy?" he asked.

Piteo shook his head.

"Because its hard to run in squares!"

"What do you get when you cross a sheepdog with a rose?" Siel asked.

Piteo tried to think but he had no idea.

"A collie-flower!" Chuckled Siel.

They both rolled in the grass, laughing so much that by the end of the day, their bellies hurt.

Other street dogs heard their laughter and joined them, soon they were all running in the grass, laughing outrageously at Siels jokes.

Piteo had the best time ever.

Afterwards, both tired, sweaty, and hungry from their adventures, Siel took Piteo to a hot dog stand.

"We are going to eat at the best restaurant in town tonight, my friend." He said, with a twinkle in his eye.

Piteo sniffed the air, the smell tickled his nostrils, it was the best his nose had ever encountered. They hovered around waiting, watching whilst the humans ate their food.

It surprised Piteo how much food humans wasted. He and Siel wasted none of it, they gulfed it down like two starving crocodiles. Piteo had never tasted anything so delicious in his life.

No one shooed them away, which was also a nice surprise for Piteo. He was so used to being pushed away by humans for hovering around food places, that whilst keeping one eye on the food he kept one eye on the action around him. Soon they were so full, they had eaten all the sausages that the humans had left on the table.

With their bellies bursting and after all the exercise they had done that day they began to feel sleepy. Siel led Piteo back to the park. They both laid under a tree and as darkness fell, they fell into a deep sleep. Piteo had always slept with one eye open in a shop doorway. That night and for many nights after, he slept with both eyes shut. For the first time ever, he felt safe.

Chapter Two
The Rescue Centre

Piteo and Siel became inseparable. They would spend their days, playing in the park, eating left over hot dogs or burgers and then fall asleep together under the stars. Siel had been an unwanted pet too and although sad, he put on a brave face. He was so cheeky and would get into so much mischief.

One day they adventured a little further, they saw a museum, with people walking in and out. They were curious.

"Come on buddy" Siel yelped. "Let's go and see."

"No Siel, you know what they say – curiosity killed the cat!" Piteo warned him.

"But we ain't cats buddy, come on." Siel said.

Piteo could not help but smile at his friend's humour.

When they reached the entrance, there was a sign on the door saying, "No dogs allowed." Siel shrugged his shoulders laughed and said,

"They don't know what they are missing buddy!" He ignored the sign and ambled straight in.

Piteo waited outside. He was so anxious. His legs had turned to jelly. He wished he could be more like his friend Siel. He would jump if a spider landed on him.

Within minutes Siel came running out of the museum with something in his mouth.

"Run, buddy" he mumbled, and Piteo, ran for his life when he saw a fat human chasing after Siel, his arms waving in the air, shouting words that were not for little doggies' ears.

When they breathlessly got to a place of safety, Siel shared his booty with his friend.

It was a sugary biscuit and was the best thing Piteo had ever tasted, better than the hot dogs. It was well worth the run they had to do to get away from the nasty man, who had stopped a while back, panting like a dog, his body bent double with his hands on his knees.

Piteo had learned something else that was new to him that day. Dogs ran faster than man. He was no need to ever be frightened again. He could outrun anyone; he felt a little more confident and a little less scared.

Siel loved his new friend, he loved him best because he laughed at his jokes. He felt so happy to have met him.

Life had suddenly got a little better for Piteo too. He now had a best friend. He had never had a best friend before. He had seen a sign once that said 'dogs are a man's best friend' – not in this case he thought. Siel is my best friend.

They loved each other; their quite different little personalities complimented each other.

The days were long and happy ones, Piteo became less anxious, he would join his friend in his cheeky antics, and they would laugh like two naughty school children, at the end of the day before falling to sleep snuggled up together in the park.

One day, things changed. They were learning that in life things cannot always remain the same. Sometimes there were sad times and sometimes there were good times. It was part of life and was part of learning.

They were playing peacefully in the park, enjoying the early morning calm before the other dogs arrived and the humans rushing to work.

The sun was hot and would get hotter as the day went on. Suddenly, a man came along. He picked Siel up into his arms. Siel struggled but the man was too strong. He began walking away with Siel in his arms.

"Hey, Mister where are you taking my friend?"   Piteo yelped, feeling much braver than he once had.

The man ignored him. Piteo did not know what to do other than to follow the man holding his friend, which he did as he tried to think how he could help Siel to escape. They walked for two hundred and twenty steps before reaching a van.

Siel did not say a word. This was unusual for him, Piteo thought, he was normally quite vocal. Perhaps he was more scared than he let on.

Piteo watched as the man gently put Siel in a small cage in the van.

Piteo barked and barked. He was not going to lose his friend, not now. He grabbed hold of the man's trouser leg with his teeth and swayed his head from left to right.

"Hey mister, give me back my friend" he barked, tears forming in his eyes.

The man picked Piteo up. He thought he was in big trouble now, but the man did not hurt him. He was put into another cage next to Siel. They both stayed silent until the van doors were slammed shut, and the van began to move.

"Where are we going?" Piteo asked Siel.

"I'll be blowed if I know" Siel replied, "but I hope its somewhere with food."

Piteo was scared, as the van stopped and started on their journey, he began to cry.

"Hey buddy, what did a Dalmatian say after his meal." Siel asked trying to cheer his friend up.

"I don't know." Piteo snivelled.

"That hit the spot!"

Piteo did not laugh this time. He was too scared. Little did he know that Siel was too.   Being a clown was just an act. Sometime in his little life he had discovered that it was not okay to show that he was scared.

They both fell into an awkward silence.   They felt every bump in the road as the van drove along at a slow speed. There was truly little room in these cages and Piteo suddenly needed to pee.

"We are still together buddy" Siel said breaking into piteos scary thoughts.

Piteo did not answer, he was too busy worrying about where they were going to end up.

The van eventually came to a halt. They heard the man get out of the cabin. The doors then opened, and the man opened each cage and put a leash on both Siel and Piteo. He lifted them out of the van and put them onto the rough concrete floor. There was no grass to be seen.

Unbeknown to Siel and Piteo they had arrived at a rescue centre for dogs. It was a place that could have a happy ending for them. A place that helped them to find their forever homes. They noticed a sealed off area and some scary looking dogs peering out at them. The man led them both towards the gates.

"Hey cuties" one of the dogs barked. "Welcome to the land of the canines."

The other dogs laughed hysterically. Siel and Piteo just looked at each other, not knowing if these bigger dogs were a friend or foe.

Chapter Three
Mrs Guardado

Siel and Piteo were led through the iron gates onto a forecourt by the van driver, who was holding their leashes tightly. He knew that street dogs would break away at any given opportunity.

All the other dogs came rushing towards them to sniff them out. This was a 'thing' with dogs. A 'butt sniff' for dogs is like a handshake for humans. They help a dog to know if another dog is male or female, how old it is, what it eats, how healthy it is and even what kind of mood they are in.

Siel and Piteo stood silently, not sure if they could be trusted or not but there were far too many of them to fight. Suddenly a loud bark took them by surprise.

"Siel, oh my God, I can't believe it, back off you lot!" He shouted at the other dogs, trying desperately to escape the arms of an elderly Portuguese woman. They all scarpered knowing that this dog meant business.

"Scruffy, is that you. Is that really you" woofed Siel. He pulled on the lead and managed to escape his handler. He ran towards the dog that he had called 'Scruffy'.

Who was this Piteo wondered, feeling, if he was honest a little bit jealous. The elderly lady put Scruffy to the floor and the two dogs rubbed noses. They were so excited to see each other.

Siel was mindful not to leave Piteo out.

"Piteo" he called, "come meet my long-lost brother, Scruffy. Scruffy this is my best friend and partner in crime, Piteo."

"Nice to meet you Piteo" Scruffy said, "my brother has led you astray no doubt."

"No, he's been really good to me" Piteo shyly replied as the other dogs burst out laughing at Piteo's unfamiliarity with Scruffy's sense of humour.

At that moment, the elderly Portuguese lady approached them with two dishes of food and two dishes of water.

"This is Mrs Guardado" Scruffy informed them. She looks after us and tries to find us 'forever homes' in England.

Neither dog was really listening. They were too busy gulfing down this delicious food before the other dogs dived in. It had not gone unnoticed that they were all licking their lips.

After lunch, Scruffy showed them around the compound, where they were to toilet, where they got fed and where they got a bath.

"No thanks, not for me!" Siel said "I don't need no bath, thank you very much, what and lose this masculine doggy smell. I don't think so!"

Scruffy smiled. He knew that once Mrs Guardado got hold of him, he would have no choice. Besides, she would then take a photo to be sent to England for nice people to look at so that they would adopt them. They needed to be suited and booted for that.

Scruffy then took Siel and Piteo to meet his friends, one of whom was just being carried in by Mrs Guardado, grunting and growling, not looking too happy as she had just had her first bath.

"This is Wally" Scruffy said.

"I smell like a blooming poodle parlour" Wally squealed, "and I got soap in my eyes." She was not happy at all.

Scruffy, Piteo and Siel, stifled their sniggers. She was so funny.

Another dog walked up to them wondering what all the noise was about and Scruffy introduced him.

"This is Jean-Luc"

Jean-Luc walked up to them all and bowed his head, like a true gentleman, that they felt sure if he had a bowler hat he would have tipped it. He then looked up at Wally and smiled.

"You are moaning again, Wally.   You look genuinely nice and smell much more pleasant."

"Tut" was Wally's only reply, snarling at her friend. Piteo and Siel watched on in awe.

"This is going to be fun!" Siel whispered to Piteo.

Later that day Wally, who seemed to have calmed down from her bath, explained to Piteo and Siel all about the rescue centre and how they tried to find forever homes for all the street dogs in countries all over the world. The four of them then went off to explore.

Piteo, was quite excited. He really loved his new friends, but the thought that one day he might have somewhere he could call home again made him feel so warm and fuzzy inside. He missed the park and the green grass, but this place was okay, I guess, and everyone seemed nice.

"Hey there" a voice squeaked, from under a sunshade. Out came a little girl doggie with a very waggy tail.

"Hi, Toffee" Jean-Luc said with a flirty pose. "Meet Siel and Piteo, they have just joined us.

"Hi Jean-Luc" Toffee said as she sauntered towards him fluttering her eyelashes. She turned to Piteo and Siel to say 'Hi'.

"Jean-Luc is my boyfriend" Toffee announced, her tail wagging so fast that they all got a blast of cool air.

"No, I'm not!" Jean-Luc snapped looking very embarrassed.

"Oh, yes you are" Toffee said.

Siel and Piteo laughed. It was obvious they were in love with each other.

The dogs were called for their tea which was chicken. Neither Siel nor Piteo had tasted chicken before. The humans tended to eat all of that for some reason. They soon learned why; it was delightful. They both felt like kings living in a 'sort of' palace. The only thing they missed was the green grass.

"It's not bad here, is it?" Siel asked when they were on their own later, we get food bought to us like the humans do."

"Yes, much better than stealing it and then having to run for our lives" Piteo replied as they joined the others in a room that Mrs Guardado called their bedroom. They even had beds; they could not believe it.

"How do you like your dorm?" Wally asked them, once they had settled in.

They both in unison replied, "it's great" and laughed. They were becoming really in tune with each other.

"There is only one house rule" Wally informed them. "No toileting in here please, we have to sleep in here, we don't want a smell!"

Siel and Piteo nodded both thinking the same, that he smelt like a dog parlour at that moment, and that was not likely to give them a good night's sleep either.

Little did they know that it was their turn the following day. Not until Mrs Guardado, came in singing "How much is that doggy in the window", swept Piteo in her arms and took him to the bathroom for a bath, followed by the beauty parlour for a trim.

When Piteo got back to the compound Siel walked right on by him. He did not recognise him.

"Hey, Siel, it's me" he yelled. Siel turned and looked surprised.

"Whoa don't you look the pretty boy" he laughed, before Mrs Guardado swept Siel into her arms singing "Puppy Love" and whisked him to the bathroom too.

Wally, Jean-Luc, Toffee and Scruffy looked on laughing out loud as Siel screamed to be put down to the floor immediately or he would ring dog-line and report her.

Mrs Guardado just smiled and carried on towards the bathroom, where Siel was given his first ever bath. If the truth be known, he quite liked it.

CHAPTER FOUR
Forever Homes

Siel came back from his bath looking very fluffy. All his knots had been carefully combed out. He seemed much calmer. He smelt soooo much better too. He felt a little uncomfortable. Mrs Guardado had said he looked cute. He was not quite sure he wanted to look cute, he quite liked his natural look.

"You scrub up nice" Toffee said.

"Oh no," he thought "I hope she's not flirting with me. Jean-Luc will not like that at all."

Everyone joined Siel and complimented him on his new look until his head swelled with pride.

Then, Jean-Luc called an important meeting, saying he had some news of great magnitude. Everyone was curious.

"When is this meeting?" Asked Wally.

"Straight after breakfast" he replied "at the back of the shed. There is a meeting room. I don't want the others listening."

Everyone gulped down their breakfast. They were all so excited to hear this news of great magnitude. As soon as they had eaten, because food always came first with doggies, they all ran to the meeting place at the back of the shed. Jean-Luc was already there.

"Mrs Guardada has found us all forever homes" he sputtered in excitement. He could not wait to share this secret information with his pals.

They all looked at each other, not sure how to feel.

"How do you know this?" Wally asked.

Jean-Luc lifted his paw and tapped his nose. A doggy sign for 'mind your own business.'

"Where are we go...going?" Piteo spluttered, feeling scared but excited at the same time if that is possible.

"Well, you are going to a lady called Linda." Jean-Luc barked. Feeling very full of himself to have this level of information.

"What about me? What about me?" They all chorused making enough noise to attract too much attention.

"Calm down and I will tell you." Jean-Luc teased. They all sat in silence, desperately waiting to hear about their new families.

"Siel you are going to a lady called Jill, who has children to play with."

Siel nodded. He tried to find a joke but could not find one. This was unlike him; he usually had a joke for every occasion. He too was scared but thrilled at the same time.

"Toffee, you are going to a lady called Angela. Wally you are going to a lady called Georgie who has a daughter called Hannah and Scruffy you are going to a lady called Candice, who has children too."

They all jumped about in excitement. Kissing each other on the noses. Wally did the highest jump in the air that they had ever seen.

Jean-Luc looked annoyed. No-one had asked about him and where he was going. He had not had chance to tell them before they began this song and dance.

Predictably, Toffee asked, as of course, she would want to be as close to Jean-Luc as she could be they were in puppy love.

"Well," he answered "it is only natural that I will be going to an especially important person. It is a man called Shaun."

"Why is he important?" Wally asked.

"He just is." Jean-Luc answered. (Secretly not knowing who he was).

At that moment Mrs Guardado came bustling in to the meeting room, waving a stick, singing "Who let the dogs out." She chased them all back into the compound.

"Why does she always sing" Wally asked Toffee as they quickly ran into the compound.

"I haven't got a clue" Toffee replied breathless. "But she can't!"

"Can't what?" Wally asked.

"Sing, of course!"

They both laughed and went for a girly afternoon together, which was far more sensible than hanging around with the boys.

Jean-Luc went for a nap. This had been exhausting. Keeping this secret had zapped him of energy. Scruffy went to spy on the girls and Piteo and Siel went to some place quiet where they could have a chat about what they had discovered today.

"Do you think it's the truth?" Piteo asked.

"Oh yes" Siel said "Jean-Luc is an oracle of information Scruffy told me."

They sat in silence for a while thinking about their new 'forever homes'.

"How do you feel buddy?" Siel asked.

"I feel good, but I feel bad too, because I might not see you again Siel."

"We will make sure we keep in touch buddy."

"How?" Piteo asked.

"Well the humans have this thing called facetime that they talk to each other on. I will sneak into Jills room and facetime you."

"Okay" Piteo naively smiled. She trusted that if there was a way Siel would find it.

Both dogs closed their eyes, they soon fell asleep, dreaming about talking to each other on facetime.

Life went on for the pooches at the Portuguese rescue centre and Jean-Luc would tell them now and again the titbits he was picking up. They were all buzzing with anxiety and waiting for any piece of news.

It was a worrying time for them. But Siel kept them occupied with his huge collection of doggy jokes.

"They are liaising with Sussex small dogs rescue about the things we need to go over to the UK, like a passport thingy and they are discussing transport arrangements, that's all I know."

He said one day when the dogs were pestering him for more news.

"How will we get there?" Piteo bravely asked him one day.

"By aeroplane, road then sea" he replied.

"Wow!" Siel said "That will be some adventure. He liked adventures.

"But what if I need a pee?" Piteo asked getting anxious as usual.

Scruffy tutted. "A puppy pad of course" he said.

"Oh" said Piteo.

He had not got a clue what one of those was and he was too scared to ask. Maybe its one of those iPads that Siel was telling him about that they could facetime on, he thought. Siel had shown him a picture of one in a magazine that Mrs Guardado read. At least he would know what to pee on now in his new home he thought.

"I must remember to pee on the ipad and not on the floor" he repeated to himself.

CHAPTER FIVE
Their adventure to the airport

One morning, they were all woken up early by Mrs Guardado. She burst into their bedroom singing "there aint nothing like a hound dog" with the collar of her blouse standing upright, a pink cape flying behind her, and her mouth twisted in a funny way. The dogs all thought it was hilarious.

"Come on, come on" she shouted "Your breakfast is ready, Mr Constancio is coming to see you all today, you need to be ready for him. He does not like to be kept waiting."

"Who is he?" they all echoed, looking at Jean-Luc the dog with all the inside information.

He shrugged his shoulders and looked away, sure that he would have spots on his tongue, or his eyes would be rolling, and they would see that he was telling lies. He knew exactly who Mr Constancio was, but he would have a riot on his hands if he told them. Mr Constancio was the local vet; he had come to do their health check and their injections needed to travel.

They were all tucking into their breakfast when Scruffy noticed that Toffee had not touched hers. She was sat with a huge frown on her forehead.

"Are you okay Toffee" he asked.   He noticed that Toffees tail was wagging at the speed of light.

"No, its my tail" she said.

"You seem exceptionally happy" Wally joined in with the conversation. "Are you excited about going to the UK?"

"No, you don't understand. My tail wags when I am happy, but when it wags at this speed it is telling me that there is something wrong."

"Wow!" Scruffy said. "I wish I had a psychic tail."

"What do you think is wrong?" Siel asked.

"I don't know, it started when Mrs Guardada told us that man was coming. There is something not right."

Everyone turned to look at Jean-Luc. They just saw the tip of his tail as he furtively left the building.

"Get your butt back here!" Scruffy shouted loud enough to bring the building down.

Jean-Luc skulked back into the building.

"What is going on with this bloke?" Scruffy asked.

"I don't know, do I?" He lied.

"I think you do" Scruffy said. His chest puffing out. "Toffee's tail is wagging like she is going to take off and fly herself to England. Talk to us we are your friends."

"Okay, okay" Jean-Luc said. "He is the vet, he has come to give us a health check so that we can go to the UK."

"Well, is that all?" Wally said. "That is nothing to get yourself in a tizzy about Toffee".

But Toffees tail did not stop wagging. There was more, she knew there was, but she dared not tell the others.

"Okay" she said and hurried away. She did not eat a morsel of her breakfast. That is unusual for Toffee because she normally liked her food.

Later that day each of them went in one by one to see the vet, Mr Constancio. They were then to find out exactly why Toffee's tail was wagging so rapidly, they all came out ooching and ahhhing. Their own tails between their legs.

They had, had a health check, a worming tablet but worst of all they had also had needles in their backsides. They all knew that Jean-Luc had known they were getting this. They ignored him all day. They were cross with him for not telling them.

The atmosphere in camp that night was horrible. Everyone sulking and moaning about their vaccinations. Siel could not stand it. He stood up and began telling jokes to cheer them all up.

"What do dogs and a cell phone have in common?" He asked. No one knew of course.

"Both have collar ID"

There was a small snigger from Piteo, even though he did not get it, but Piteo always laughed at Siels jokes.

"Why was the dog such a good storyteller?" He continued.

"He knew how to paws for effect."

That one got a few sniggers.

"What do you call a dog magician?"

"A Labracadabrador"

They all laughed at this one. The mood was beginning to lighten.

"What is a dogs favourite instrument?" He asked. No one answered.

"A trom-bone" he laughed, and they all laughed too.

"I know one, I know one" Jean-Luc shouted up, hoping that a good joke would help the dogs to forgive him.

"What does a dog say before eating?" He asked, a grin on his face. No one knew.

"Bone appetite!" He rolled with laughter, all the other dogs did too.

This went on for most of the evening. Each dog delivering a joke, until they were all rolling around the floor in hysterics.

Wally laughed that much she thought she was going to pee. Most of them ended up laughing at her belly laughter than at the jokes. They were all friends again and Piteo was pleased about that. He hated an atmosphere.

Days passed and everyone was getting on like a house on fire. Jean-Luc was forgiven they knew he had not told them about the needle, with a good heart and they learned how important the treatment was, for them all to travel to the UK.

One day, much to their surprise Jean-Luc ran up to them breathless to give them some further news.

They all gathered around excited wondering what Jean-Luc was going to say.

It was amazing to hear that they were all flying over to Lisbon the following day, where they were being taken by a pet transport van to Calais in France and they were catching a train that went in a tunnel under the sea all the way to the UK, where they would be meeting their new families and going to their forever homes.

Piteo was nervous, it had been such a long time since he had lived in a family home. Deep down he really needed a human to love and who would love him too. He like his doggy friends but they were unable to rub his tummy like human hands did. Doggy paws just scratched him.

That night none of them could sleep, they lay awake excitedly talking all night about what their new families could be like.

"I hope mine are rich and can buy me lots of bones" Scruffy said.

"I hope mine has a park nearby to take me on walks" Piteo added, remembering the park he and Siel used to play on.

"Well, mine is bound to have a hot tub, I can soak in with a glass of bubbly." Toffee said, her nose in the air with an air of grandiose.

This went on and, on all night, all discussing their imaginings, hopes and dreams. But, mostly hoping they were loved.

Jean-Luc assured them that they would be loved so much because the rescue centre in the UK checked the humans out to make sure that they were nice people. They even did a home visit to ensure they had a safe home.

The following day they silently ate their breakfast all were starting to feel nervous. They knew it would be a long journey as Jean-Luc had told them. Two and a half days he had said. None of the doggies thought it would be that long.

Mrs Guardado came outside to wish them goodbye. She was hugging them, so hard they could not breathe. Tears fell down her face.

"Adeus menus amigos" she said, which was 'Goodbye my friends' in Portuguese. They felt sad to be leaving her. She had been good to them and fed them well too.

Piteo wanted to tell her to get some grass in the compound and then it would be like a first-class hotel. They would all come back for a holiday then.

They all licked her face, which was more to stop her strangling them with her hugs than anything else.

Before they could say whiskers, the van was there, and they were all being loaded on. They went into separate cages but could still see each other and speak to each other. They were pleased about that.

Once they were all in the van, the other dogs barked 'goodbye and good luck'. The back doors were shut after one final wave from Mrs Guardado and they were on their way. Another new adventure that would take them to their new families, their forever home.

CHAPTER SIX
Back at the compound

The van travelled along the road at a lulling pace, which sent the doggies to sleep very quickly. They had spongy and cosy beds to lie on as they snuggled down for the first leg of their journey.

They were very tired as they had slept little the night before. There was a soft sound of music coming from the radio that was soothing and relaxing, accompanied by a rhythmic sound of subtle snores.

The excitement mixed with anxiety had exhausted the team of six. They were like a football team heading for the finals, on a Saturday afternoon.

In the meantime, their families in the UK, who had spent the final few days getting everything prepared for them, were getting excited too. They had been counting down their sleeps and for them it was only two more sleeps. The children were struggling to sleep too, they were too excited and so eager to see their forever friend.

Some of the dogs had been given English names as well as their Portuguese names. Siel was going to be called Arthur and Piteo was 'Piteo Marley Spencer'. They felt incredibly special having more than one name.

About a million steps later the van pulled to a halt and the drivers got out. The doors shutting woke the dogs from their deep slumber.

"We are here" Toffee said nervously.

None of them could believe they were going on an aeroplane they had never been on one before. It was both frightening and breath-taking to know that they would be flying thousands of feet in the air.

"Will we be able to chase the birds." Piteo had asked them all one evening. They had all laughed and explained to him that they would be in the cargo hold, inside the plane and that if there were any birds they would be outside the plane.

They waited and waited to be moved from the van to the plane, it seemed like forever. They could hear voices outside of the van but could not quite make out what was being said. Then they heard a man with a raised voice who seemed to be talking on the telephone because they could not hear the other person responding. It was all very strange.

"Oh God, my tail is wagging ten to the dozen again" Toffee cried. "There is something wrong."

They all looked at Jean-Luc.

"Don't look at me!" he said, "I am as clueless as you lot."

"Are you sure?" asked Scruffy "because if you are lying to us again, I will bop your nose. This is no joke now."

"No, honestly I know nothing." Jean-Luc did the sign of the cross on his heart, which in doggie language meant that he was telling the truth.

"Oh, calm down." Wally said. "They are probably sorting everything out. It takes time these things."

They sat for a long time waiting and waiting. Then the men got back into the van, started the engine, and began driving again.

"See, he is probably driving us to the plane now" Wally reassured them. They all settled down again, except Toffee whose tail was almost spinning around now. They sat in silence for a long while until Siel said.

"It's a long way to this blooming plane."

They all agreed, but there was nothing they could do, they were in the back of a van with no view out of any windows.

Toffee started howling.

"What on earth is the matter Toffee?" Scruffy asked. "You are bursting my ear drums".

"I am trying to make them stop, and open the doors to investigate, so at least we will then be able to see out the back of the van at where we are going."

It was an ingenious idea, but it did not work. The drivers had their music on too loud.

There was nothing more they could do but sit and wait.

Eventually, after an awfully long time, the van pulled up again. The drivers jumped out of the cabin and opened the back doors.

"Wait I recognise that smell!" Jean-Luc announced. They all nodded. They knew the smell too. They were back at the compound.

One by one they were taken out of the van, all the other dogs looked at them in shock, as they made their way to their bedroom. Exhausted and deflated.

"What do you think has happened?" Siel asked Jean-Luc.

"I don't know but I intend to find out!" Jean-Luc responded and bounced off in the direction of the office.

What the other dogs never knew was that Jean-Luc had a secret hiding place where he could eaves drop on everything that was going on.

The van drivers followed Mrs Guardada into the office and the conversations began. Jean-Luc listened intently through the air vent.

Back in the UK, their new families were just getting out of bed, thinking "only one more sleep now."

They were so happy, until their phones started to ping with messages telling them that their 'forever friends' had not got on the flight.

There were tears and confusion both in the Portuguese rescue centre and in their family homes in the UK. Everyone was devastated.

The staff at the rescue centre were devastated too, this was the first time anything like this had happened. Their day was full even before it had officially started.

Piteo sat snuggled up to Siel, he was holding back his tears. This was overwhelming for him. They had spent half a day in a van and arrived back where they had started. He like all the dogs were in shock.

Mrs Guardada brought them all in some warm milk in their bowls, which they lapped up gratefully.

Jean-Luc came back had got them all to gather around. Even some of the other dogs joined them to hear Jean-Luc's findings. They were all curious to know what had happened.

Jean-Luc coughed before he began, anxious himself to tell the story.

"Well" he began. "Everything was booked, the pet transport van was waiting in Lisbon to take us to Calais and then on to the UK. Our families were all ready to pick us up. But when we got to the airport there was no booking. Someone had booked it on the internet but not pressed the correct button to confirm and so there was no booking for us on the flight."

"You just can't get the staff these days" Scruffy piped up.

"Who was it?" Siel asked.

Jean-Luc stayed silent. He may be a snoop, but he was not a snitch.

"Mrs Guardada!" Wally, Toffee and Scruffy all shouted out at the same time.

Jean-Luc said nothing. His nothing said it all.

"So, what happens now." Piteo shyly asked.

"The rescue company in the UK are spending the day trying to rebook the pet transfer for another day, but that won't be easy because they are all quite booked up. They will let Mrs Guardada know later today. The worst thing is they have lost all the money that they paid the pet transfer company at Lisbon. So they have to pay again."

"Oh, Lordy" Scruffy said, "Are they going to do it?"

"Yes" Jean-Luc responded.

Piteo burst into tears.

"Why are you crying?" Siel asked "That's good news."

"It's j…jus…just that they really must want us." He stuttered.

"Yeeeeh" the whole room chorused. They barked in celebration. They really were loved.

"What did our families say?" Toffee asked.

"I bet they are upset" Wally said "I hope mine are okay"

"I wonder what mine are thinking" Scruffy asked.

"The eight-year-old little girl, said "that's okay Mummy as long as Scruffy is safe, that is all that matters."

Tears slid down Scruffy's fluffy face. This was so unlike him, like his brother he always kept a brave face. "They must really love us" he sobbed,

"They are all trying to help in any way they can, they are even fundraising to recover the rescue centres loss." Jean-Luc replied.

"Oh, I love them already." Toffee cried.

"Piteo your new Mummy is an author, and she is even writing a book about us to raise funds."

"Wow, will I be in it." Piteo asked.

"Yes," Jean-Luc said, "we all will."

"We are going to be famous!" Toffee shrieked, her tail wagging in happiness. "Its not turned out such a bad day after all." She said.

They all laughed and went for a doggy nap, this adventure had well and truly worn them out. They fell into a sleep dreaming of their new homes, all feeling the warmth of the love of the UK rescue centre and their families.

CHAPTER SEVEN
The Journey to the UK and their forever homes

The following morning Jean-Luc was up early, he had even skipped his breakfast to sit by the air vent to pick up any news that he could about a planned reschedule of their trip.

He had heard that Shaun had said that he would get a van and go and fetch them all himself. He swore that if he did this, he would do his housework forever!

Everyone was doing their best. Jade, Maggie and all the staff at Small Dogs Rescue in Sussex had been on the phone all day, trying to get a pet rescue van and book another flight/

It had not been easy. They were all exhausted. Jean-Luc could not believe they would all do that for them, he was overwhelmed with gratitude.

"English people are so kind" he thought.

The other five doggies had moped around all day, not building their hopes up too much, as they were used to disappointment in their incredibly sad lives already.

Jean-Luc stayed at his watch and listen spot until teatime and was starving hungry by the time he returned to the compound with some news. But for the first time in his doggy life food did not come first!

He bounced up to his pals, full of excitement, hardly able to contain his joy.

"They did it! They did it!" he yelped.

Wally, Toffee, Scruffy, Siel and Piteo gathered around him, their little hearts in their mouths. Not daring to hope for the best.

"They got us a van, they only went and done it!" He shrieked.

"When?" they all asked, hoping for a bit of rest between journeys. They were eager to go, but still exhausted from their previous trip.

"12 days!" Jean-Luc told them.

"Yeh!" they all shouted. Jumping in excitement. That would give them plenty of time to recuperate and be raring to go on their next adventure.

They danced around the compound and all the other dogs ran to see what all the fuss was about. Putting their thumbs up once they heard the news.

There was dancing and joy all day in the Portuguese rescue centre. Mrs Guardado even threw them some special meaty bones to celebrate.

"It's a bit like Groundhog Day" she said.

"Don't you mean 'Hound Dog' Day" Siel laughed. All the other dogs did too. Mrs Gaurdado looked confused. She did not understand doggy language. Not all humans did.

In the meantime, whatsap messages were pinging away in the UK to all the adoptees who had been anxiously checking their phones all day. They were informed too that a reschedule had been arranged. They were elated and the children cried with joy.

And so, the countdown began again. 12 sleeps, 11 sleeps, 10 sleeps and so on until the journey began again. This time going smoothly, thanks to Sussex Small Dogs Rescue Centre and their staff.

None of the dogs were as nervous as they were first time around because they knew their families in the UK loved them soooo much now.

The van picked them up again, this time they made it to the plane. They were put into a hold and all the stewards chatted to them and made them feel at ease. They could not see each other, but they could still talk to each other.

"I hope this is first class" Toffee said out loud, to whoever was listening.

"Only the best for you honey" Jean Luc answered.

"Siel can you hear me" Piteo said.

"Yes I can hear you buddy, are you okay?"

"Yes, I'm having the best time, soon I am going to be flying in the air whoosh!"

When the plane landed in Lisbon they were transported to another van and driven down to Calais. They slept for most of that journey, tired out after the excitement of their flight.

They arrived at Calais and drove onto the train that would take them under the sea to England. It was such a great adventure.

Eventually Scruffy, Wally, Toffee, Jean-Luc, Siel and Piteo arrived safely at their pickup point in the UK, exhausted but relieved. It had been a long journey. But they were here.

The van driver got out of their cabin and opened the doors.

"The UK smells nice" Siel whispered to Piteo.

"It sure does" Piteo replied.

"I smell burgers, do you?"

"Yes" Piteo replied.

"Let's go get 'em buddy" Siel barked.

But before they could make a dash for it, a safety leash was put on them, a collar, dog coat and lead with a tracker on the collar, by the pet transport guys.

"Boy, they sure don't want to lose us" Siel yelped across to Piteo.

"That's nice though, isn't it?" Piteo asked.

"Yes, I guess it shows we are loved and cared for." Siel agreed, but it still did not stop him wanting one of those burgers though. They smelled soooo good.

"English burgers smell so much nicer than Portuguese ones buddy." He said.

"Yes they do, Siel" Piteo said, as the man was putting his collar on. It felt strange he was not used to having a collar on his neck.

When the dogs got out of the van, they were led to their family and handed over to them with all their documentation.

"Hey, stop cuddling me" they all heard Jean-Luc say "I am not that type of guy. Besides, I need to get to know you first."

They all laughed. They knew that this was his macho streak that he put on in front of them. They knew he would be lapping up the attention once they were out of sight. Just like he did with Toffee.

Most of them had seen them sharing a bone and licking each other the night before promising to love each other forever.

Siel and Piteo were handed over to their new owners, who began to lead them away.

"Hold fire buddy" Siel shouted pulling onto his leash. He turned to Piteo and said "You be brave Piteo."

"Yes, I am Siel, thanks to you and all that you taught me. I will miss you!"

"Me too buddy" Siel replied, a tear in his eye.

"Facetime me Siel"

"Will do, Buddy".

Piteo heard Siel say,

"I hope you're stocked up on burgers Mrs, I have an acquired taste you know."

Piteo laughed. Humans didn't understand our language and wouldn't know what Siel was saying.

They both were led away by their new owners to another new place for another new adventure. But this time it was forever.

Piteo

Thank you
Sussex Small Dog Rescue
for all that you do.

For parents

It is estimated that in 2020, there were roughly 9.8 million dogs in the UK. Whilst most of these dogs are much loved members of their families, thousands of dogs find themselves in dog pounds and rescue centres each year.

The Dogs Trust estimate that there are roughly around 110,000 dogs needing rehoming at any one time. Rescue centres across the country are consistently running at or above capacity. If you are thinking about bringing a dog into your life it makes sense to consider adopting a rescue dog instead of buying a puppy.

Taking a rescue dog into your family can be a little more challenging and it is vital that new owners do whatever they can to ensure that their rescue dog adapts well to its new and loving home as quickly as possible.

By choosing to adopt a rescue dog, you are saving the life of an animal that relies upon humans for care and shelter. You will be giving them a fresh start and a new home, and in return you will get unconditional love.

Many rescue centres rely totally on fundraising. Even if you are unable to adopt a rescue dog, by buying this book you are supporting Sussex small dog rescue in rescuing, supporting, and finding homes for homeless dogs throughout the UK and abroad.   Thank you.

I would like to personally thank Sussex rescue centre for allowing me to adopt Piteo and for going to all lengths to get him over to the UK from the Azores. As you can see it was not an easy journey, but they went above and beyond to ensure these doggies got to their loving families and have a forever home, at a considerable financial loss to themselves.

A dog is for life. He is your friend, your partner, your defender, your dog. You are his life, his love, his leader. He will be yours, faithful and true to the last beat of his heart. You owe it to him or her to be worthy of such devotion.

Sussex small Dogs rescue own the copyright to this book and all proceeds will go to them.

I dedicate this book to two beautiful dogs Milly and Piteo.

Printed in Great Britain
by Amazon

63303948R00047